MY BOYFRIEND IS A MONSTER

I Love Him to Pieces

#1

OR

MY DATE IS DEAD WEIGHT

OR

HE ONLY LOVES ME FOR MY BRAINS

EVONNE TSANG

Illustrated by JANINA GÖRRISSEN

GRAPHIC UNIVERSE™ · MINNEAPOLIS · NEW YORK

STORY BY
EVONNE TSANG

ILLUSTRATIONS BY
JANINA GÖRRISSEN
ADDITIONAL INKS BY MARIA VILLAR

LETTERING AND COVER COLORING BY
ELDON COWGUR

Copyright © 2011 by Lerner Publishing Group, Inc.

Graphic Universe™ is a trademark of Lerner Publishing Group, Inc.

Graphic Universe™
A division of Lerner Publishing Group, Inc.
241 First Avenue North
Minneapolis, MN 55401 U.S.A.

Website address: www.lernerbooks.com

Library of Congress Cataloging-in-Publication Data

Tsang, Evonne.
    I love him to pieces / by Evonne Tsang ; illustrated by Janina Görrissen.
       p.   cm. — (My boyfriend is a monster ; #01)
    ISBN: 978-0-7613-6004-9 (lib. bdg. : alk. paper)
      1. Graphic novels. [1. Graphic novels. 2. Interpersonal relations—Fiction. 3. Zombies—Fiction.
    4. High schools—Fiction. 5. Schools—Fiction. 6. Chinese Americans—Fiction. 7. Saint Petersburg
    (Fla.)—Fiction. 8. Horror stories.] I. Görrissen, Janina, ill. II. Title.
    PZ7.7.T8Ial 2011
    741.5'973—dc22   2010030774

Manufactured in the United States of America
1 – DP – 12/31/10

3

DRIP
DRIP
DRIP

5

8

14

15

16

24

31

34

49

SUNDAY.
2 P.M.

VVVVRRRRRR

VVVVVVRRRRRRRRRr

RRRRRVVVVVVRRRRRRRRRRRRVVVVVRR

VVVVVVRRRRRRRRRRRRRRRRRRRRR

55

YES...

YES...

OK...

SPEAKERPHONE'S ON.

JACK, YOU HAVE SOME SORT OF "PLAN"?

MY PARENTS LEAD THE CDC TEAM HANDLING THIS INFECTION.

MY PARENTS DIDN'T WANT ME IN THE GENERAL EVACUATION. THEY HAVE FEDERAL AGENTS IN ST. PETE COMING TO GIVE US A RIDE OUT.

HOW LONG WILL THAT TAKE?

I DON'T KNOW. THE AGENTS WILL CALL WHEN THEY'RE CLOSER. THE OUTBREAK HASN'T REACHED DOWNTOWN YET, SO WE'RE SAFE FOR NOW.

FOR NOW.

MR. BELL, I'LL MAKE SURE DICEY IS SAFE.

DICEY? YOU THERE?

I LOVE YOU TOO, DADDY.

TELL JOEY TOO, OKAY?

I'M GLAD YOU GUYS WILL BE SAFE IN TAMPA.

BYE.

JACK, I'M SCARED.

ME TOO.

AM I MISTAKEN, OR DID YOUR DAD ALREADY KNOW YOU WEREN'T AT SCHOOL?

ALL RIGHT, I GOT PERMISSION.

DITTO YOUR MOM, KNOWING.

WE'RE THE LAMEST DELINQUENTS EVER.

68

97

98

109

110

116

MISS BELL, DO YOU NEED MEDICAL--

JACK!

JACK!

CLANG

JACK.

MISS BELL.

MISS BELL, IT'S BEST TO LET THE DOCTORS CHEN WORK IN PEACE.

THEY'RE JACK'S PARENTS?

YES. ARE YOU INJURED?

I SLAMMED AGAINST THE DOOR WHEN I SIDESWIPED A PALM TREE.

IT DOESN'T HURT THAT--

I NEED MEDICAL HERE.

DICEY!

JOEY?

JOEY!

DADDY!

DICEY!

DICEY!

DICEY!

DICEY!

123

PELICAN POST
ST. PETERSBURG HIGH SCHOOL

Transcript of a live chat with Dicey Bell and Jack Chen. Six months after the zombie apocalypse, the heroes from St. Pete answer readers' questions.

IHEARTCHEESE: Has your life changed since you got famous?

DICEY: Not really. The military cleaned up St. Pete pretty fast. It's a little weird to be doing normal senior year stuff, I guess.

JACK: There's the free ice cream.

DICEY: Oh, yeah! Emperor Penguin said we could have free ice cream for a year! That's pretty awesome.

JACK: They already regret it. Dicey could out-eat an elephant.

JACK: Dicey has her bat, so I'm just going to change that to: her athletic, svelte figure seems immune to thousands of calories of ice cream.

PARKER09: is it tru ur dating?? ++++romantic!!!

DICEY: I'm too busy eating ice cream to date.

TENNISFAN7: Jack, what was it like to be infected by the zombie fungus? Any leftover side effects?

DICEY: The brain damage seems permanent.

JACK: I'm fine! The fungus never reached my brain. And yes, we're dating!

TRUFFLEBUNNY: How could a fungus turn Jack into a zombie?

JACK: I am not a zombie.

JACK: *Cordyceps* fungus attacks insects all the time. It takes over the little insect brain and makes the bug climb out on a tree branch where the fungus spores can spread a lot more easily. In the mutation that attacked humans, the spores were concentrated in the mouth. So it turned out that the mutation spread best through bites.

DICEY: Spores in the mouth.

DICEY: You didn't tell me that.

JACK: But it didn't spread through kissing. I guess.

TRUFFLEBUNNY: Should I stop eating mushrooms?

JACK: You can keep eating mushrooms. My family used to cook with dried *Cordyceps* all the time, just like any other tasty fungus.

DICEY: You didn't tell me that.

SPARKLESRHOT: So what's it like dating a zombie?

DICEY: There's a difference between a zombie and a high school boy? Well, when you get a zombie's attention, you know that it'll stick with you, at least until it can eat your brains. Regular guys are more fickle.

JACK: I AM NOT A ZOMBIE!

Category: Interviews, Chat Transcripts
Tags: apocalypse, brains, cordyceps, dating, eating, fungus, zombies

ARTIST'S SKETCHBOOK

DISEÑO DE PERSONAJES

Para diseñar los personajes el autor me envía una descripción de ellos en la que me tengo que basar. No tanto el aspecto físico—ése se describe rápidamente, y a no ser que haya detalles importantes (p. ej. piercings o tatuajes) no hace falta más. A veces los autores me nombran a actores como ejemplo de cómo se imaginan los rasgos generales de sus personajes, cosa que resulta muy útil.

Pero sobre todo quiero conocer el carácter del personaje, sus aficiones, su forma de ser . . . Todo ello puede influir en el diseño.

Normalmente, la cara del personaje queda bastante definida desde el primer boceto, ya que si no me gusta, lo borro y lo modifico. Aún así muchas veces vuelvo al primer boceto.

Supongo que como tantas veces en la vida, la primera impresión es la que se queda.

CHARACTER DESIGN

To design the characters, the author sent me a description of them to work from. Not so much the physical side—that can be described quickly, and unless there are important details (for example, piercings or tattoos), that's all that's needed. Sometimes authors name actors as examples of how they imagine the general features of their characters, which is very useful.

But above all, I want to know the personalities of the characters, their hobbies, their way of life.... All this can influence the design.

Normally, the character's face is pretty clear from the first sketch. If I don't like it, I erase it and modify it. But, many times I return to my first sketch.

I guess, as is so often true in life, it's the first impression that matters most.

—Janina

ABOUT THE AUTHOR
AND THE ARTIST

EVONNE TSANG is a native New Yorker who attended high school in zombie-apocalypse epicenter St. Petersburg, Florida, before returning to the Northeast to earn a BA in English with a minor in creative writing from New York University. At NYU she was editor in chief of the science fiction and fantasy magazine. Her previous book for Graphic Universe™ was Twisted Journeys® #12, *Kung Fu Masters*.

JANINA GÖRRISSEN was born in Frankenthal, Germany, and studied comic arts in Barcelona, Spain. Her works include the shojo manga *Kairi* (published in France by Les Humanoïdes Associés) and *Black is for Beginnings* from Flux. Her website is jgoerrissen.com.